SuperCat
vs the chip thief

Jeanne Willis

Illustrated by Jim Field

HarperCollins *Children's Books*

First published in Great Britain by HarperCollins *Children's Books* 2014
HarperCollins *Children's Books* is a division of HarperCollins*Publishers* Ltd,
77-85 Fulham Palace Road, Hammersmith, London W6 8JB

Visit us on the web at
www.harpercollins.co.uk

3

SUPERCAT VS THE CHIP THIEF
Text copyright © Jeanne Willis 2014
Illustrations copyright © Jim Field 2014

Jeanne Willis and Jim Field assert the moral right to be identified
as the author and illustrator of this work.

ISBN 978-000-751863-0

Printed and bound in England by
Clays Ltd, St Ives plc

MIX
Paper from
responsible sources

FSC
www.fsc.org   FSC C007454

CONTENTS

Chapter One
TOXIC SOCK SHOCK

James Jones looked at the tubby tabby snoring on his bed and sighed. The cat was fast asleep on his school jumper and James was already late. "Up you get, Tiger," he said.

He shoved his hands under the cat's saggy tummy to lift him. Tiger pinned himself to the pillow, made a fat, furry arch and wouldn't let go. James put his blazer on.

"Fine, I'll catch cold," he said. "Sleep, eat, poop! That's all you ever do. If Mum had bought me a pet wolf like I asked, at least I'd have someone to play with."

James had always wanted an exciting pet. It didn't have to be a wolf. He'd have been happy with a polar bear. Or a panther…

But he didn't get one of those. Instead, he was given a cat from the rescue centre.

It was a gift for his seventh birthday. He was so excited when his mother handed him the cardboard pet carrier. He couldn't wait to see what was inside. He could hear loud purring, so he guessed it wasn't a python. Maybe it was a lion cub? Or a cheetah? He opened the lid. Inside was...

"Are you pleased?" said his mum.

James looked at the roly-poly puss in the box. The cat opened one

eye, blinked at him and went straight
back to sleep.

"Can I swap it for a crocodile?"
begged James. "I promise to take it
for walks."

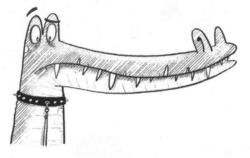

But three years later he was still
stuck with the world's laziest cat.
Tiger was cuddly and lovable, but he
hardly moved.

He didn't want to go in goal:

Or pretend
to be a spy:

Or have a
sword fight:

Not even for
a chicken leg.

James tried his best to bring out Tiger's wild side. He even named him after his favourite superhero, but while Tigerman was full of get up and go, Tiger the cat only got up to go to his litter tray. Or his food bowl. Or back to bed.

James didn't give up. He dressed as a lion tamer to make Tiger do circus tricks. Fat chance! Tiger looked at him as if he was mad, curled up on the stool and wrapped his tail over his eyes.

Once, James pretended he was an Indian prince with a real pet tiger that

liked to be taken for walks around
the palace garden. He clipped his little
sister's old reins to Tiger's collar, but
when he went to lead Tiger outside, the
cat just sat down. He refused to move.
James dragged him along on his furry
bottom, but Tiger slipped his collar
and James found himself walking with
nothing on the end of the reins.

Maybe he could teach Tiger to hunt. Tiger had never caught a mouse in his life, but there was always a first time. James found a sausage in the fridge, tied it to a piece of string and ran round the garden with it.

"Chase it, Tiger!" he cried. "Chase it!"

Tiger rolled over in the rhubarb patch and stuck his nose in the air. James thought he'd sniffed the sausage and was about to pounce – but no. Tiger stood up, curled his tail into a question mark and ambled back to the bedroom.

To be fair, Tiger didn't spend all of his time on James's bed. Sometimes he went *under* the bed. It was the place where James liked to keep dirty plates, along with his comics and caterpillar collection.

If Tiger was lucky, he might find a piece of pepperoni from an old pizza. Or some burger gristle. Or a lump of cheese. So as soon as James left for school, Tiger rolled off the bed to see what he could find below.

He picked his way through a sea of
last month's pants. His nose twitched –
what was that smell? Aha… it was an
oven chip – his favourite! It was stuck
to a mouldy sports sock by a blob of
lard. Tiger licked it.

The greasy, cheesy chip-sock combo was delicious. He took such a big bite that he chewed a hole in the sock heel. He was enjoying it no end until suddenly a bit of wool went down the wrong way.

He tried to cough it up but no matter how hard he retched, it stayed put. His eyes bulged. Thinking he was about to choke, he gave a loud GULP! and swallowed hard.

That moment changed Tiger's nine lives forever. As he lay on his back looking up at the bedsprings, the mouldy sock shred dissolved in his stomach. Tiger felt a strange sensation. His fur stood on end. His whiskers fizzed. His paws tingled. Fit as a kitten, he shot out from beneath the bed and sprinted up the curtains.

They sagged under
his weight.

Just before the pole
snapped,

he gave a giant leap and…

...landed on top of the wardrobe.

Tiger sat there in shock. He couldn't understand how he'd got there. The curtains were on the other side of the room. He'd never jumped that high or that far before. It was an impossible leap for an ordinary cat – so maybe he wasn't an ordinary cat any more! This morning, he hadn't had the energy to wash his bottom – but now?

I wonder if I can fly, thought Tiger, flapping his furry arms.

He fell off the wardrobe into the laundry basket with a loud *plop*.

Normally, if he fell off something he slept where he landed. This time, he sprang up and dusted himself down.

"Maybe I'm dreaming," he said. "Whoa, I can *talk*! *C'est fantastique!*"

He clapped his paws over his mouth.

"Not only can I talk, I can speak French! I wonder if I can sing."

He cleared his throat and burst into song.

"There was a farmer had a dog, his name was Bobby Bingo,

B – I – N – G – O, B – I – N – G –
O, B – I – N – G – O,

His name was Bobby Bingo!"

Tiger couldn't believe what had just come out of his mouth.

"Not only can I sing, I can spell. Excuse my French, but *Je suis incredible*! I wonder if I can play James's guitar."

Standing on two legs, he went to pick it up.

"Hey, I can walk like a man!" he whooped. "*Fabuloso!* Oh – now I'm speaking Spanish! In which case,

27

I bet I can get a good tune out of this instrument."

Tiger plucked the strings. They made a pleasing *twang* and, before he knew it, he was strumming away and headbanging to the beat.

"Wild thing, you make my heart ping!

You make everything... gravy!"

He was about to sing the second verse when he realised that it was impossible for a cat to play a guitar unless... He stopped and examined his paws.

"I've got thumbs!" he sang. "I can talk, walk, sing, dance. I play the guitar… I'm a *Supercat*. I wonder what else I can do!"

By noon, Tiger was thrilled to find that he could do lots of things that people could do. Even better, he was as strong as a lion and as fast as a cheetah. Timing himself on James's stopwatch, he worked out he could reach his food bowl in twenty seconds. It took twenty minutes before. He sucked in his tummy and puffed out his chest.

"However shall I use my amazing new powers for the best?" he wondered.

He picked up one of James's comics and flicked through it for inspiration.

"*Tigerman versus Count Backwards and the Calculator Crew*," he said. "This is a good story. Flaming furballs – I can read!"

As he learned about Tigerman's heroic attempts to defeat his enemy, Count Backwards, Tiger knew what he had to do.

"I will be a crime fighter and rid the

world of evil!" he said. "Which means I need a costume fit for a superhero."

He flung open the wardrobe, put on some clothes and studied his reflection.

"I am not sure that these Y-fronts go with the space helmet," he said, giving them a tweak. "They're a bit baggy."

He did a karate kick and they fell down to his ankles.

"I need something that fits me like a glove," he said. "And it would be nice if it had sequins."

James's sister, Mimi, went to ballet. She had lots of shiny dancewear. Tiger stroked his chin thoughtfully.

"I wonder if she has a leopard-print leotard," he muttered to himself.

Armed with a pair of scissors, he raided her chest of drawers…

Later that afternoon, Supercat – once known as Tiger – posed in front of the mirror. He was very pleased with the outfit he'd made from Mimi's leotard and a pair of old pants.

He pulled his tail through the hole he'd cut in the seat, put on his mask and swished his cape.

"*Magnifico!* I look the cat's whiskers in this," said Supercat, strutting about like a treacle pudding in tights.

He couldn't wait for James to get home from school so he could show off his new outfit. He looked at the clock. It was half-past three.

"I have half an hour to kill before James arrives. I must make myself useful."

With super-feline speed, Supercat began to tidy the bedroom. He'd done nothing to help James in the past and he thought it would be a nice surprise.

But it was more than a surprise. It was a total shock. When James

walked in, he found his pet cat
sweeping crisp crumbs into a dustpan
– and he was singing!

"There was a farmer had a dog,
its name was Bobby Bing—"

"Tiger…" gasped James.

Supercat swung round.

"*Bonjour!*" he said. "How was
your day? I thought I'd give your
room a spring clean. I bet you don't
recognise the old place."

James didn't recognise the old
cat. He rubbed his eyes. Tiger took
his school blazer and hung it up – or

was it Tiger? It had to be – he had the same wonky whiskers.

"Tiger, you've... changed," he said.

Supercat did a twirl.

"I look stunning in this costume, don't I?" he said. "It's got 'go faster' stripes..."

James pinched himself... Ouch! No, he wasn't dreaming. His cat was wearing a hilarious home-made superhero outfit and was talking to him.

"You look pale," Supercat said. "Did you skip school dinner?"

James's knees buckled. The last thing he remembered before he fainted from shock was a loud *twang* as he fell and hit the guitar.

Chapter Two

THE CHIPS ARE DOWN

When James came round, he found himself sitting on the edge of the bed with his head between his knees.

"What happened?" he said.

Supercat pressed a cold flannel to his forehead.

"You fainted."

James had guessed that much.

"No, what happened to *you*, Tiger?"

Supercat shrugged. He didn't like to mention that he'd swallowed a slimy sock.

"*Je ne sais pas*. Which, in case you don't know, is French for 'I don't know'."

James stared at him in disbelief.

"How do you know French? You're a cat."

His pet tabby pointed proudly to the letters S and C on the front of his outfit.

"I'm not just any old cat. I'm Supercat!"

40

He lifted the wardrobe
with one paw to show
his incredible strength.

At that moment, James
knew it was true – his cat
had superpowers.

He jumped up and down on the bed in excitement.

"Supercat, this is brilliant!" he said. "Think of all the fun we can have together! Why didn't you tell me you could do all this amazing stuff before?"

"I only found out myself this morning," said Supercat.

James wanted to know everything.

"What happened? Was there a flash of lightning and everything changed?"

"Maybe it was something I ate," Supercat said, mysteriously. "All I know is that I am now more tigery than Tigerman. I'd soon have that evil Count Backwards on the run."

James's mouth fell open.

"You've been reading my comics? Cool! Tigerman's the best, isn't he?"

"Tiger Power, rargh, rargh, rargh!" It was Tigerman's catchphrase. "I was thinking of using it if we find ourselves in mortal danger," Supercat said.

"*We?*" said James. "You and me?"

"Of course you and me! If I'm

going to rid the world of evil, I'll need

you by my side. Every superhero

needs a sidekick."

James filled with pride.

Then his face fell.

"But I haven't got any superpowers."

"No, but you're super-intelligent,"
said Supercat. "You got gold stars for
sums and spelling, didn't you? That
could come in very useful."

James couldn't see how knowing
nine times nine and being able to spell
'Mississippi' were going to defeat
many villains, but he didn't care. He
just wanted to find out what other
amazing things Supercat could do
before Mimi came back from ballet.
Mimi must never know about his
superpowers. She'd tell Mum and Dad
and they'd ruin everything by saying

James was too young to hang out with a superhero.

Right now Dad was asleep after working the night shift in his cab. James and Supercat creeped past his bedroom and sneaked out into the garden. James fetched his pogo stick and bounced up and down on the patio.

"It's easy once you've got your balance," he said. "Want a go?"

He held the pole still while Supercat stood on the pegs.

"I'm not sure this is a good idea,"

said Supercat, wobbling violently.

"You'll be fine," said James. "Just keep your paws on the pegs, hold tight and jump."

Supercat bent his knees, did two little jumps and then…

he went into orbit,

bounced off the roof

48

and pinged right into

the next-door garden.

James ran over to a hole in the fence and looked through. Supercat was face down in a compost heap with his cape over his head.

"Are you OK?" he called.

Supercat picked the mouldy grass clippings out of his fur and answered in German.

"*Ja!* The spring in the pogo stick was stronger than I thought."

"*You're* stronger than you thought," said James, as Supercat scrambled back over the fence.

James wanted to test out

Supercat's skills some more but Dad would never forgive him if they smashed the greenhouse window or broke the fence.

"Maybe we should go to the park," he said. He grabbed his cricket bat, ball and stumps. "Bring the skateboard too if you like, Supercat."

Supercat peered at the plank of wood on wheels, his whiskers knitted in confusion.

"Just stand on it like this and kick yourself along," said James, giving him a quick demonstration. "Your turn."

Supercat stepped on to the end of the board, but he used so much force, it flipped up in the air, somersaulted right over his head and smacked him on the bottom.

YEE-OW-WOO!

"*Yee-ow-woo!*" he shrieked.

Taking care to stand on the

skateboard gently this time, Supercat
sped off to the park, leaving a trail of
scorch marks on the pavement.

"Wait for me!" puffed James,
running after him.

By the time he got to the park,
Supercat was playing on the swings.
Luckily there was no one else around.

"I wouldn't go so high if I were
you!" warned James.

Too late. The swing seat flew
backwards over the bar in a great
circle that got smaller and smaller
as the chains wrapped themselves

around it. When it finally stopped,
Supercat was dangling upside down
with his cloak trapped in the workings.

"Give it a tug!" called James.

Supercat yanked the material.
There was a ripping noise, the cloak
slipped free and Supercat plummeted
down.

James caught him in his arms and
fell with Supercat on top of him. They
lay there nose to nose.

"Have you damaged anything?" said James.

"Yes… my cloak!" said Supercat crossly.

James was just glad he wasn't hurt.

They got up and, as James held the cricket stumps, Supercat hammered them into the ground with his furry fist.

"Great teamwork," said James. "You bat, I'll bowl."

He soon regretted it. He kept forgetting how powerful Supercat was and, as he aimed for the wicket,

57

THWACK! – Supercat hit the ball over the trees and right out of the park. James watched in amazement as it disappeared over the horizon.

THWACK!

"I'm not fielding that!" he said. "It's probably landed in Holland. Now what?"

Supercat completed his hundredth run, leaned on his bat and rubbed his tummy.

"Eat!" he said. "They've got tuna sandwiches in the park café."

The café was on the other side of the lake about 100 metres away.

"How do you know they've got tuna?" said James.

Supercat licked his lips.

"I can see them through the window with my super-feline vision. Actually, the crusts look stale. Fancy fish and chips instead?"

They were James's favourite, but it was a long walk to the chippy.

"If you give me the money, I'll run and get them," said Supercat.

James sighed.

"They won't serve cats."

"Why not?" sulked Supercat. "My money is as good as anybody else's."

Desperate for cod in batter, he came up with an idea.

"I'll borrow your dad's cab. He's asleep. The car keys are in the fruit bowl. He won't miss them."

By now, James was really hungry for chips.

"Can you drive?" he said.

"How hard can it be?" said Supercat. "I'll pick you up by the park gates."

James waited. He only lived around the corner and after ten minutes he was worried that Supercat might have run someone over. Just then, he saw the cab.

For one awful second James
thought it was his dad – the driver
was wearing his cap – but to his relief
it wasn't. Supercat wound down the
window. He was sitting on a pile of
road maps.

"Sorry I'm late," he said. "I couldn't
see over the steering wheel."

James got in and they drove off, singing along to the radio.

"Take a left at the lights," he said.

When they arrived, Supercat parked outside the chip shop and sniffed the air.

"Mmmm! I'll have cod, chips and a battered sausage please."

"Try and make yourself invisible until I get back," said James. "In case a policeman sees you."

"Invisible?" said Supercat. "I'm not sure that's one of my superpowers, but I'll have a go."

He squeezed his eyes shut and clenched his buttocks in an effort to disappear.

"Have I gone yet?"

"Supercat... Supercat? Where are you?" said James.

Supercat's eyes snapped open.

"That's odd," he said, patting his own knees anxiously to make sure he still existed. "I'm here! How come I can see me but you can't?"

"Just joking." James grinned. "You're not really invisible. Back in a bit."

As James went to get the food, Supercat ducked down in the driving seat with a big smile on his face. Even if he couldn't make himself invisible, this was the best day ever.

But suddenly it took a turn for the worse. James returned empty-handed.

"I don't believe it!" he said. "Chips cost twenty pounds a bag in there. Why are they so expensive all of a sudden?"

Supercat started up the car.

"Let's try another chip shop. They might be cheaper."

65

They drove into town and found one. Again Supercat gave James his order and again James came back chipless.

"They're *twenty-five pounds* a bag in there and there are none left," he said.

Supercat was so disappointed.

"None? Can't they make some more?"

James shook his head.

"The man said there's a potato shortage."

Supercat thumped the steering wheel.

"There will be a cat shortage in a

minute – I'm fading away! Was there
any cod?"

James got back in the car.

"No. They can't make chips
without potatoes, so there's no point
frying fish. They're closing down
because they have no customers."

"I'm a customer!' said Supercat.
"Have they got nothing to eat at all?"

James felt in his pocket.

"I got you this pickled egg."

Supercat crammed it into his
mouth. His whiskers drooped over
his bulging cheeks.

"Urgh – *dith-guth-ting!*" he said.

He pressed the electric button to lower his window and spat it out. Chewed egg splattered on the glass.

"You opened my window, not yours," said James. "Let's go home. I'll open a tin of pilchards for you instead."

Supercat held up his thumbs.

"Excuse me. I can open my own."

The journey back was easy.

Getting the car on the drive without

being seen was not.

"Uh-oh! Mimi's spotted us," said

James. "She'll tell Dad."

"Let's pretend you were driving,"

said Supercat. "I scraped the

paintwork."

"I'm ten… it's against the law," said James. "How can we shut Mimi up?"

"What would Tigerman do?" asked Supercat.

"He'd fool Mimi into thinking she *imagined* you were driving," said James. "Act like Tiger in front of her. If she knows you have superpowers, she'll use it against me."

He opened the front door.

"Remember to behave like an ordinary cat," he whispered.

"I've forgotten how," said Supercat.

James pointed to a large potted plant in the hall.

"Pee in that fern."

Supercat looked at him in disgust.

"Is that what Tiger did?"

"Every day," said James. "Now try not to talk."

Supercat squatted in the pot. Just then, Mimi came running down the stairs. She wagged her finger at James.

"Um! I'm telling Daddy you let Tiger drive his cab."

"You need glasses," said James. "Tiger can't drive."

Tiger flicked a speck of fluff off his leotard.

"He's right, I can't," he said. "I almost hit a lamp—"

"Shh!" hissed James.

Mimi clapped her hands over her mouth.

"Tiger can *talk*!" she squealed.

"You're hearing things," said James. "You poor little mad girl."

Mimi stamped her foot.

"I am not *little*! I'm telling Daddy you drove his cab unless you do as I say."

She looked Supercat up and down.

"Who made Tiger's costume – was it you, James?"

"N… Yes," he said.

Mimi gave him a wicked smile.

"Then I only won't tell Daddy if you make me a dress for my dolly."

James had no choice.

"OK," he groaned. "But promise not to tell."

"Cross my heart," said Mimi. "But you have to make matching knickers!"

Supercat's pilchards would have to wait.

Chapter Three
CHIP WARS

It was Saturday morning. James and Supercat had stayed awake all night talking about chips, cats and comics. It was breakfast time and they were still at it…

"James, is Tigerman's costume better than mine?" asked Supercat.

He was so pleased with it, he'd worn it to bed.

"No, just different," yawned James. "Shall we have a quick snooze? We might need to do some crime fighting later. There's something fishy about the price of chips, I can feel it in my bones."

"I can feel it in my stomach," said Supercat. "I bet some rotter is behind it!"

He leaped out of bed.

"Where are you going?" asked James.

Supercat dropped to the floor and did fifty press-ups.

"Tigerman didn't get to be a superhero by snoozing," he said. "He was always up and ready to protect the universe from evil Count Backwards."

"'Know your enemy!'" said James. "That was his motto."

Supercat had read lots of *Tigerman* comics last night, but one thing still puzzled him.

"I can't think why the Secret Service let Count Backwards work for them in the first place," he said. "He's as mad as a bag of nuts."

James sat up. He was never too tired to talk about his favourite comic-book characters.

"Count Backwards wasn't always mad," he said. "He was brilliant at maths. The Secret Service hired him to solve the hardest sum in the world to crack an enemy code. It's all explained in the first story."

"I haven't read that one," said Supercat.

James fished under the bed and pulled out a box. Inside was the very first *Tigerman* comic.

"It's in mint condition," said James. "Have you got clean paws?"

Supercat held them up for inspection. James brushed off the cat litter.

"OK," he said. "You can read it now."

At the beginning, Count Backwards looked quite normal. Supercat hardly recognised him. In the comics he'd seen, his whole face and body were tattooed with numbers and ugly sums.

"He's still sane in this picture," said James. "See? He's smiling. After twenty years, he finally cracked the impossible sum."

"That's 140 in cat years!" said Supercat. "No wonder he looks happy."

James nodded.

"It didn't last. Before he had a chance to save the answer on his computer, the cleaner pulled out the plug and it was lost forever."

"All that hard work for nothing?" said Supercat. "No wonder he went nuts."

James flicked the pages over.

"He threw his computer out of the window and went on the rampage, messing with people's numbers."

Supercat scratched his head.

"What numbers?"

"Door numbers," said James. "Phone numbers. Lottery numbers.He even stole the numbers off the town clock."

"No wonder the Secret Service fired him," said Supercat.

He shuddered at the picture on the back page. It was Count Backwards escaping from prison.

"The thought of that maniac on the loose is enough to put me off my food… almost," said Supercat, heading out of the door.

"Where are you off to?" said James.

"My super-feline ears tell me your dad has just opened the fridge," he said. "I'll get him to make my breakfast. Tigerman always had a big breakfast before he went into battle."

James waved at him frantically and called him back.

"What's up?" said Supercat.

"*You* are!" said James. "You're walking on two legs. You have to behave like Tiger in front of Dad or you'll blow your disguise. Take your costume off."

Supercat pulled a sulky face and stepped out of his pants.

"I look silly with no clothes on," he said.

"You've looked sillier," said James. "I'll be down as soon as I've got dressed."

By the time James came downstairs, Supercat had already eaten his breakfast and was talking to someone on the telephone.

"Tiger can't come to his appointment today," he said. "He's busy. Cancel it."

He slammed down the phone.

"Who were you talking to?" said James, panicking.

"The vet," said Supercat. "And I've rung every chip shop in the phone book, but no one's answering. I don't like the sound of it one little bit."

Supercat's ears began to swivel.

"There's a very interesting report on the telly," he whispered, dropping on to all fours. James followed him into the front room to listen.

"… According to farmers, millions of potatoes have been destroyed by a plague of strange grubs. Potatoes are now so rare, they cost more than gold."

"No wonder the price of chips is so high," James murmured.

"There'll be no mash with my bangers soon," said Dad. "No shepherd's pie, no roasties on Sunday."

"It won't end there," said Mum, turning up the volume on the telly.

A reporter stood in front of a large map.

"If the grubs spread worldwide, there will be no potatoes left to make babkas in Russia, gnocci in Italy or hash browns in America. And in Israel there will be no latkes at Hanukkah. When the chips are down, countries with no potatoes may invade those that have some, which could lead to spud wars..."

"Spud wars?" said James. "This is serious. Where did the grubs come from?"

"It's where they're going to that bothers me." said Dad. "I should drive

to Murphy's Farm and dig my spuds
up now before they're destroyed."

"You haven't got time," said Mum.
"You've got an airport run in ten
minutes."

"I'll dig them up for you, Dad,"
said James. "I'll ride to the plot on my
BMX. It might be our last chance to
have chips!"

He winked at Supercat, who ran
upstairs, sneaked his costume out of
the house and got dressed behind a
bush. James was waiting for him in the
alley with his bike.

"I'm all ready for action!" said

Supercat.

"Your pants are back to front," said

James.

"I wondered where my tail had gone," said Supercat, swivelling them round. "So, given that I'm as fast as a cheetah, do you want to pedal or shall I?"

"It's a no-brainer," said James, standing on the stunt pegs.

He put his arms around Supercat's chubby waist and held on tight.

"Tiger Power, rargh, rargh, rargh,!"

They were off!

Chapter Four

ROOT OF ALL WEEVIL

It would have been quicker to cut through town, but a cat riding a bike might have caused a commotion so they went the long way round.

Supercat pedalled at such speed down the lanes that James was worried the tyres might melt. They

reached Murphy's Farm in no time.
All they had to do now was tackle the
steep hill that led up to Dad's little
vegetable patch.

"You might have to change gear,"
said James.

Supercat frowned.

"Why? Don't you like this outfit?"

"I meant shift the gear on the bike,"
laughed James. "It might be easier to
go uphill in fourth."

It was *too* easy for a cat with
superpowers. As they approached the
top of the hill, Supercat showed no

signs of slowing down. In fact, he was speeding up.

"Look out!" warned James.

"I can't," said Supercat. "My mask's slipped."

The eyeholes were now round the back of his head.

James clung on for dear life as the bike launched into the sky. Supercat pedalled helplessly in the air, then the bike tipped forward, hit the slope and bounced across the grass like a bucking bronco. James jumped off and rolled to the bottom, but Supercat

BOING

kept going...

and going...

and going…

"Brake!" shouted James.

Supercat gave the lever a hard
squeeze.

"Tiger Power, rargh, rargh...
aargh!"

The bike threw him off and he
flew through the air until – *SPLASH!*

He landed in a horse trough full of
slimy green water.

James helped him out, trying not
to laugh.

"Are you OK?"

Supercat wrung out his cape and
put it back on.

"Tigerman never worried about a drop of water," he said. "I shall drip dry."

He waved his paws like jazz hands.

"Fetch me a spade. Imagine how fast I will dig with super-paws!"

James unlocked his dad's shed. He fetched a short shovel for Supercat, sacks and a bucket.

Supercat's digging skills were amazing. The potatoes flew out of the ground so fast James had to run at top speed to catch them in the bucket.

He picked up the few he had
missed, brushed off the mud and put
them in a sack.

"No sign of weevil holes," he said.
"These will make lovely chips."

"Mmm… mmm!" said Supercat.

"You're dribbling," said James.

Supercat wiped his chin on his cape. He stopped digging and stared up at the sky. James noticed that his ears were swivelling again.

"What can you hear?"

"Whatever it is, I don't like the sound of it," growled Supercat.

James strained to listen. Nothing.

"You're imagining things."

Then he heard it too. *Pocka-pocka-pocka-pocka-pocka...*

Out of nowhere, a helicopter buzzed across the plot. It flew right over their heads, swooping so low

that the blades blew

Supercat's whiskers flat.

James read the name and

number on the undercarriage:

Busta Crackdown 54321.

"Run!" cried Supercat.

They raced to the shed and ducked down. James peeked through the window. The helicopter was hovering over the next vegetable plot.

"It's dropping something," he said. "Are they bombs?"

Supercat's eyes grew wider and wider. Using his super-feline sight, he could see that these were no ordinary bombs. They were balls of manure loaded with wriggling, twitching grubs.

"Weevil bombs!" said Supercat.

They hit the ground and exploded, scattering weevils far and wide.

The gruesome grubs
burrowed underground,
searching for potatoes
to scoff. Supercat thrashed
his tail.

"Someone is
deliberately destroying
the crops. Who would
do such a wicked
thing?"

BOOM

James pulled out a pencil and paper.

"This is no time to play Hangman!" said Supercat. "There are steak and chips... I mean chips at stake!"

But James wasn't playing. The name on the helicopter was bugging him. He licked the end of the pencil and wrote the letters down: BUSTA CRACKDOWN.

He didn't know of anyone called Crackdown. Yet the name sounded familiar. He moved the letters around:

COWARD SNACK TUB.

WON BACK CUSTARD.

Supercat peered over James's shoulder.

"'Coward Snack Tub', 'Won back Custard'… What nonsense is this?"

"It's not nonsense," said James. "'Busta Crackdown' is an anagram – a word hiding in another word. If I use the same letters to make a new name, it will tell us who the pilot is."

"So!" said Supercat. "He disguised his name because he's up to no good?"

"Exactly," said James. "I've cracked it!"

He spelt it out on the dirty window with his finger. Supercat's whiskers shot up.

"COUNT BACKWARDS!"

James went pale.

"The number on the helicopter was 54321. It's the Count's favourite catchphrase. It must be him, but *how*? He's just a character in a comic!"

"Maybe that's just want he wants us to believe," said Supercat.

As the pilot leaned out of the cockpit, Supercat's eyes went into sharp focus. He recognised the face straight away. It was covered in number tattoos.

"Unless my super-feline eyes deceive me, it's him all right, as large as life and twice as ugly. We have to stop him!"

They watched as the helicopter

dropped more weevil bombs.

It swung round and came thundering towards them.

"Retreat! He might be armed," yelled James as they ran back.

Ack-ack-ack-ack-ack! The Count pelted them with stinking weevil bombs.

Supercat flicked a blob of manure off his costume.

"He spattered my sequins! *No one* gets away with that!"

"Let's bring his helicopter down," said James.

He pulled up a
cabbage the size
of a football
and threw it
to Supercat,
who caught it and
wrinkled his nose.

"James! You know I hate cabbage."

"Don't eat it. Throw it at the
helicopter!" said James.

Count Backwards thumbed
his nose at them and turned the
helicopter round.

Supercat did some knee-bends.

He rolled his shoulders. He flexed his
paws.

"He's getting away!" yelled James.

"Oh no, he's not!" said Supercat.

He sped after the helicopter. He
stopped. He spun round
and round like a
discus thrower

CHOP

and hurled the cabbage into the
blades.

BAM!

It shredded like coleslaw. The
helicopter zigzagged like a swatted
fly.

"Good shot, Supercat!" said James.
He grabbed his BMX. "Let's go after
it!"

Chapter Five

ONE POTATO, TWO POTATO

"You pedal, I'll steer," said James. "Just in case your mask slips again."

He stood on the stunt pegs and held the handlebars while Supercat pumped the pedals. They shot off after the Count's stuttering helicopter,

113

the wheels sparking like Catherine wheels.

"Faster!" yelled James.

He took a sharp left.

"He's heading for the golf course."

Supercat did a wheelie as the helicopter went into a tailspin. It disappeared behind some trees.

"It's going down!" said James.

They waited for the crash. But there wasn't one. They pedalled through the woods to investigate.

"That wasn't there before!" said James.

There was a strange little castle
in the clearing. It was no wider than
a caravan but as tall as a house.
It had turrets and flags, but unlike
any castle James had ever seen,
it had a chimney and a porch.

As he screeched to a halt in surprise, Supercat shot over the handlebars and landed head first in a golf bunker.

"Sorry," said James, helping him up. "I thought cats always landed on their feet."

Supercat rubbed the sand out of his eyes.

"I performed that super-move on purpose," he said. "Where's the helicopter?"

It had landed on the castle roof.

"There's Count Backwards!" he said. "He's climbing down the

chimney. We must go and arrest him."

"Not so fast," said James. "We don't know what's inside."

They crept over to the castle. James parked the bike on the porch. There was a name over the front door: Buck Daconstraw.

"Buck Daconstraw?" said Supercat. "Never heard of him."

James mixed up the letters in his head.

"Oh, I think you have," he said. "It's none other than Barack Downcust – I mean Count Backwards.

This must be his headquarters."

"I knew it," said Supercat, "as soon as I saw the numbers 54321 on the flag."

He went to knock on the door. James held him back.

"Shouldn't we take the Count by surprise? Tigerman always does."

"Good thinking," said Supercat. He glanced to the top of the castle. "Let's shin up the drainpipe and drop down the chimney."

James looked at Supercat's podgy waistline and then at the narrow chimney.

"Let's not."

"Why not?" said Supercat.

"Um… I hate heights," said James,
trying to spare Supercat's feelings.
"There must be another way."

There was a basement window at the back of the castle. It was just big enough to climb through, but it was locked.

"I'll smash it," said Supercat, picking up a hefty rock.

James waved his arms in alarm.

"Drop it! We don't want the Count to hear us... *Ouch!*"

"Shh, the Count will hear us," said Supercat.

James hopped up and down.

"You dropped it on my foot!"

"*Pardonnez-moi,*" said Supercat.

"I'm such a butter-paws."

James tried to ignore his throbbing toe and studied the window frame.

"If I had something sharp to remove the putty, I could lift out a pane of glass."

Supercat unsheathed his super-claws.

"James, I have something sharp."

He ran his fore-claw round the putty and the pane came loose. They laid it carefully on the grass.

"I'll climb in first," said James.

He crawled through the gap and

landed softly in the cellar.

"Hurry," he whispered.

Supercat was dangling half in, half
out of the window.

"Come on. Don't be a scaredy-cat," said James.

Supercat fixed him with a hard stare.

"I'm not scared. My tail hole is caught on the latch."

James unhooked him. He stuffed his fist in his mouth to stop himself giggling.

"It's not funny," said Supercat. "I could have ripped my... Oh! I hear footsteps."

James looked round anxiously.

"Quick! Hide under the stairwell behind those boxes."

They hid just in time. The door
burst open and a troop of men
marched down the stairs with heavy
sacks slung over their shoulders. Their
uniforms were covered in sums.

"Are they who I think they are?" mouthed Supercat.

James nodded.

"It's the Calculator Crew. They work for Count Backwards," he whispered.

Supercat remembered their sickening behaviour in issue 6 of *Tigerman*.

"They're pure evil," he cringed. "I wonder what they've got in those sacks."

He peeked out from behind a box. One of the Calculators pulled on a metal ring in the floorboards – there was a trapdoor.

"Bung 'em down here, lads!" he commanded.

The Calculator Crew slit open their muddy sacks and emptied them. As the contents rumbled into the hole below, they sang:

"One potato, two potato, three potato, four,

Five potato, six potato, seven potato, more."

Supercat couldn't believe his ears.

"There are a lot more than seven potatoes in those sacks. There must be seven million. Those Calculators can't count for toffee."

More men came. They tipped potatoes down the hatch until it was full. Then they picked up any spuds

that had gone astray and stuffed
them down their socks.

"I'm having mash tonight, Mr Minus,"
said Mr Plus. "Don't tell the Count!"

"I'm having croquettes, Mr Plus," said
Mr Minus. "Keep it under your hat."

They closed the trapdoor and left. When the sound of their footsteps had disappeared, James and Supercat came out of hiding.

"Why is Count Backwards storing all these potatoes and destroying the rest?" said Supercat, hunting round to see if the Calculators had missed any.

James shrugged. "If he's got the only potatoes left in the world, he'll make a fortune selling them. But knowing him, he'll have a much madder plan in mind."

"Whatever it is, we have to find out," said Supercat.

There was a low, rumbling noise.

"Was that your tummy?" said James.

Supercat cupped his ear.

"No… but my super-feline hearing tells me it's an engine starting up."

There was a loud *clunk-clunk*, *clunk-clunk*, like the sound in a jet when the landing gear drops down. It was coming from underneath them. Now the walls were vibrating. The room shook so hard it rattled the potatoes against the trapdoor.

"The earth's moving!" yelled Supercat. "Earthquake!"

James looked out of the window. Trees and buildings flashed past. He grabbed on to the sill to steady himself.

"It isn't the earth that's moving," he said. "It's the castle!"

Supercat clung to the curtains and peered out. The scenery whipped past.

"Clumping cat litter!" he screeched. "The castle's on wheels!"

There was no getting away from it.

Count Backwards' HQ was motoring across the fairway at 100 kilometers an hour, scattering squirrels, startling deer and scaring the birds. And they were trapped inside.

"He's driving like a maniac!" shrieked Supercat.

"He *is* a maniac," said James. "Hang on! We're in for a bumpy ride."

Chapter Six

ONE–DERFULLY SMELLY

The motor castle left the golf
course and screeched round the
back lanes.

If a tractor or truck appeared, the
castle parked and pretended to be a
building. When the other vehicle was
out of sight, it zoomed off again.

"I wonder where we'll end up,"
said James.

"I hope it's a burger bar," said
Supercat. "I've missed so many meals,
my costume's gone baggy."

The elastic in the pants looked as if
it was about to snap, but James didn't
like to mention it.

"A bargain bucket of fried chicken
would be nice," sighed Supercat.

But Count Backwards' HQ didn't

stop anywhere near a fast-food place.
It went along an old railway track.
Past the docks. Across the wasteland.

"It's slowing down," said James.

The castle came to a halt near a
fleet of helicopters.

"It's parked by an old ketchup
factory," said James. "Wacko's Cut
Brand."

"Good," said Supercat. "I like
ketchup."

Wacko's Cut Brand? James had
never heard of it. He mixed the letters
up and scowled.

"CURT BACONDAWKS? Aha! COUNT BACKWARDS! The factory must belong to him."

It was heavily guarded by the Calculator Crew.

"Whatever he's making in there, it's not tomato sauce," said James.

There was a terrible smell coming from a massive metal skip.

"My super-feline nose tells me it's horse poo," said Supercat.

"I could have told you that," said James.

Supercat folded his arms and

looked a bit cross.

The castle door opened and Count
Backwards appeared, followed by
more members of the Calculator Crew.
Some had empty sacks.

Some carried spades.

The Count pointed to
the manure heap.

"Get shovelling,
lads. Five, four,
three, two, one-
derfully smelly!"
he said.

The Count gave a ghastly grin and went back inside the factory.

The Calculator Crew climbed into the skip and began bagging up the manure.

"This job stinks," said Mr Plus.

"It gets right up my nose," said Mr Minus. "But don't tell the Count."

"I'll give you one guess what he's doing with all that manure," said James, watching as the Calculators carried the full sacks into the factory.

"Putting it on his rhubarb?" said Supercat.

"No, making weevil bombs," said James.

"Let's spy on him!" said Supercat.

James hesitated.

"Hang on… how will we get past the guards?"

"I don't know," said Supercat. "You're the brainy one."

Just then James spotted the perfect opportunity.

"Fancy a brew and a bicky, Mr Plus?" said Mr Minus.

"I'll join you in the canteen, Mr Minus," said Mr Plus.

They wiped their hands on their uniforms and went for a tea break.

"Now's our chance," said James. "We can hide in a sack."

There was one by the skip. The Calculators had left it half-filled.

"You're joking," said Supercat.

But he wasn't. James waited until the guards weren't looking, then he ran over to the sack and held it open.

"In you get, Supercat!"

Supercat took a step backwards.

"I'm not sure my superhero outfit is safe to put in the boil wash."

"Tigerman is never afraid to get his hands dirty," said James, jumping in.

Supercat held his nose and climbed after him. They crouched down in the bottom of the sack. James sprinkled manure over their heads until they were hidden.

"The Calculators will think the sack is full of poo and carry us in," he said.

"One of us is full of poo," grumbled Supercat. "And one of us has to clean his fur with his tongue!"

It was warm and steamy in the sack. Supercat dozed off. Ten minutes later, James gave him a nudge.

"The Calculator Crew are coming back from their tea break."

Supercat woke up. His head was muzzy.

"Where am I?" he said. "Is it night-time?"

"No," said James. "We're in a sack full of… shh!"

Supercat squinted through the holes. He saw two pairs of boots covered in numbers.

"My back is killing me, Mr Plus," said Mr Minus. "But don't tell the Count."

"As you gave me a ginger nut, I'll give you a hand, Mr Minus," said Mr Plus.

They tied up the sack and swung it into the air. They carried it into the factory with James and Supercat inside. Bump, bump, bump up the stairs.

"I feel a furball coming," squeaked Supercat. "A big hairy one."

His body stretched and shrank like a concertina. He started to retch.

"Swallow it!" said James. "They'll hear you!"

Supercat clamped his paws over his mouth. His cheeks ballooned. His eyes watered.

"Has it gone?" whispered James.

Supercat stroked his throat and gulped.

"Yes… No… Not sure…"

Mr Plus stopped walking. A metal door opened.

"On the count of three, throw the sack, Mr Minus," said Mr Plus.

"Three, two, one… heave, Mr Plus!" said Mr Minus.

The sack slid down a chute…

and landed at the
bottom. Supercat
clawed a hole…

and he and James
climbed out.

They were in a storeroom full of sacks of manure. No one was around.

"You can bring up your furball now," said James.

Supercat tried, but nothing came out except a super-feline burp.

"It's got stuck in my U-bend," he said.

James grabbed him by the paw.

"Let's go. Look out for the guards."

They ran up the stairs and down a long corridor. There was a room at the end. A sign on the door said 'DO NOT ENTER'. James looked through the

glass panel. Inside was a laboratory
with rows of huge plastic tanks inside.
They were full of fat, wriggling grubs.

"So this is where Count Backwards
breeds his weevils," said James.

"The swine!" growled Supercat.

His ears pricked up. He could hear the *clank*, *whoosh* of machinery coming from above.

"That must be where he makes the bombs," he said. "Let's catch him in the act."

"Then what?" said James. "Count Backwards won't give up without a fight. There are only two of us. We don't stand a chance against the Calculators."

Supercat did a high-kick and chopped the air rapidly with his paws.

"You seem to forget that I have a

150

black belt in salami."

"Isn't salami a sort of sausage?" said James.

"I wish!" said Supercat. "In fact, salami is an ancient form of feline fighting. It was the sport of Egyptian kings. It is extremely deadly."

He flew through the air and prodded the 'up' button on the lift with his toe.

"Have no fear, Supercat is here!" he said.

"It's too risky to take the lift," said James, sending it back down. "It'll be guarded – you can't fight salami-style in a tight space like that. We need to find another way."

There was a panel in the wall. He pulled it open. There was a ventilation pipe inside, just big enough for a boy and a fat cat to crawl through.

"It must lead to the top floor of the factory," said James.

"After you," said Supercat.

"After you," said James. "You can see in the dark."

It was pitch-black inside. There were a lot of twists and turns. James felt as if everything was closing in.

His heart was racing. He stopped still.

Supercat kept walking ahead, chattering away, but when James didn't answer, he suddenly realised he was far behind him.

"It's no good. I can't do it, " called

James, trying to back out on his hands and knees.

Supercat tried to turn round to fetch him but the tunnel was too narrow, so he reversed until he bumped into him.

"Never fear, Supercat is here!" he said.

"Your bottom is in my face," said James.

155

"It's OK, I'm wearing pants," said Supercat. "Hang on to my tail. Off we go! You can do anything when we're together."

James inched forward and grabbed hold. Even though Supercat was pulling him along at top speed, the tunnel seemed to go on forever.

"We will get out of here alive, won't we?" he said.

Supercat did his best to jolly him along.

"Tiger Power, rargh rargh rargh!" he said. "James, I've been wondering. Do you think I need a new catchphrase?"

At that moment, James didn't care.

He was struggling to breathe.

"I can't keep using Tigerman's," said Supercat, hoping to take James's mind off things.

"How about,

157

'Is it a bat? Is it a rat? No, it's Supercat!'?"

"That's silly!" laughed James, forgetting to be scared "How about, 'I've earned my stripes!'?"

"Not bad," said Supercat. "Or how about, 'Hang on to your hat, it's—'"

"Look!" said James. "We're nearly there."

He could see daylight.

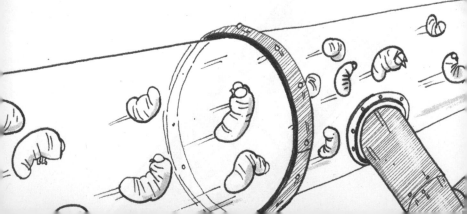

Supercat dragged
him along to the end
of the pipe, then
they both dropped
down silently on
to the balcony.

They could see
right into the
factory below.

A stream of grubs flowed through a tube into vats of manure. The manure was then squirted into weevil-bomb moulds on a conveyor belt. When they reached the end, they were tipped into barrels and taken away on trolleys by the Calculator Crew.

"They must be making thousands of bombs a day," whispered James. "We have to stop the production line."

Suddenly, Supercat spotted Count Backwards sniffing one of his own bombs.

"Five, four, three, two, one-derfully explosive!" snickered the Count, rocking the bomb like a baby. "I will destroy every potato in the land! There will be spud wars. People will be fighting over the last chips and the Secret Service will have to sort out the chaos. That will teach them to get rid of me. How *dare* they say my mind had turned to mash! I will make them eat their words, but they will never eat chips again! Ha ha haaaaa!"

Never eat chips again? Supercat filled with rage. Before James could

stop him, he spread his claws and
threw himself over the balcony.

"Hang on to your hat, it's Supercat!"
he yelled, aiming for the Count.

Count Backwards looked up at
the oddly dressed tabby hurtling
towards him...

and only just managed to roll out of
the way.

"Good catchphrase, bad move!" he screamed. "Seize him! Your days are numbered, Supercat!"

Chapter Seven
DOG FIGHT

While James gave the Calculators
the runaround up and down
the fire escape, Supercat put up a
good fight. He held off nine crew
members with his lightning-fast salami
moves. Then somehow his cape got
caught in Mr Plus's belt.

In the kerfuffle that followed, Mr
Minus grabbed Supercat round the
tummy, squeezed hard and the furball
shot out.

It landed on Mr Plus's lip and stuck
there like a snotty moustache.

Supercat stopped fighting and started to laugh. As he rolled about giggling, Mr Plus lifted him up by the scruff of his neck.

"Look what the boy's dragged in, My Lord," he said.

Count Backwards pulled Supercat's mask forward and pinged it.

PING

"Well, now. Who do we have here? Is it Tigerman's chubby infant daughter?"

Supercat pointed to the S and C on his costume.

"Respect the letters!" he spat. "This is no Babygro!"

Count Backwards patted him on the head.

"I must clip your claws," he laughed. "Five, four, three, two, one down, one to go! Somebody grab that scrawny lad."

James was so worried about

Supercat, he was caught off guard by
Mr Minus and hauled in front of Count
Backwards.

"Got him, My Lord!" said Mr Minus.
"He's a slippery little devil."

The Count flicked James on
the nose and counted
his freckles.

"Five, four,
three, two,
one too
many for my
liking! Your
number is up!"

James kicked and struggled.

"I know what you're doing. I'll tell the Secret Service!" he said.

Count Backwards clutched his sides and chortled.

"Small potatoes! They're powerless to stop me. I'm blackmailing them for the enormous sum of five, four, three—"

He stopped mid-speech and glared at the furball stuck to the Calculator's lip.

"You need a close shave, Mr Minus! Tie that brat up with his moggy, then come to my chamber. I will trim your moustache with my cut-throat razor."

"You will never get away with this!" said James as the Calculators bundled them away.

"Do the maths!" called Backwards. "Me divided by one fat cat plus one small boy? It's never going to happen. You must multiply your efforts by 9.8088796544 x 803,478.8976 to defeat me!"

"Your arithmetic is mental!" said James. "Good always triumphs over evil."

Count Backwards did a crazy dance towards him.

"But not over *weevil*," he said. "I'll weevil-bomb every country in the world, starting with France! At five o' clock, I'll fly across the Channel and begin my attack."

He lobbed a weevil bomb over the banister.

"They won't know what's hit them!" he sang. "They will be fighting over French fries by beddy-byes if I've done my sums right!"

He began to sob hysterically and

curled up on the floor.

"And I *did* do my sums right, Mummy!"

"Why are you doing this?" yelled James as the Calculators dragged them to the basement.

"You're so selfish!" said Supercat.

Count Backwards dabbed at his eyes and called down the stairs.

"Me… *selfish*? I cracked the hardest sum in the universe. I should be a hero! But no, the Secret Service left me to rot. Sweet potatoes, I will get my revenge!"

The Calculators wrestled their prisoners into a dark room and tied them to a chair.

"Ouch! He scratched me, Mr Plus," said Mr Minus.

"The cat?" said Mr Plus.

"The boy," said Mr Minus. "My

finger's gone puffy. I'm allergic to boys."

"Come, I'll fetch you a plaster," said Mr Plus. "I'll draw a smiley face on it."

They slammed the door and left. James tried to wriggle free, but the rope was too tight.

"How will we ever get out?" he cried.

"You've only been here for five minutes," said a sulky voice. "I've been here for five months. I'm bored out of my enormous brain."

Through the dim light, James saw
a short man with a long beard tied to
another chair in the corner of the room.

"Professor Sprout," said the man.
"Chief scientist for the Secret Service."

"How did you end up in here?"
asked James.

The professor sighed deeply.

"I was kidnapped by Count
Backwards. He's holding me to
ransom until the Secret Service pays
him a billion pounds."

Supercat went into a yoga position
and nibbled at the rope around his paws.

"That's blackmail!" said James.
"But why did the Count kidnap you instead of someone really important?"

"I *am* really important," grunted the professor. "I'm the world's expert on weevils. He forced me to breed a

potato pest that multiplied faster than any other. If I refused, he threatened to have me mashed, boiled and fried."

Supercat bit through the rope and leapt out of his chair.

"Ta da!"

He began to untie James with his super-feline thumbs.

"If only I wasn't such a genius," groaned the professor. "But I created those potato-munching weevils and I'm the only one who can stop them."

"How?" said James, as Supercat loosened the knots around his wrists.

"I can breed a bug that will eat them all," he said, clicking his fingers. "I could save the potatoes just like that! But until the Secret Service pays Count Backwards his billion, my hands are tied."

Supercat whisked the rope away.

"Not any more, Professor! You're free to go."

Professor Sprout twiddled his fingers.

"Marvellous! I must get to work at once."

He went over to the door.

"Locked," he tutted. "Has anyone got something pointy to open it with?"

Supercat showed him his super-feline claws. They looked like Swiss Army knives.

"Take your pick, Professor," he said.

Sprout pointed to the middle claw and Supercat jiggled it in the keyhole. There was a click, then the door swung open. They all ran out.

"Not so fast!" said the guard, grabbing the professor by the beard. Professor Sprout screamed like a lady. In a flash, Supercat dropped to the floor, tied the guard's bootlaces together and nipped his ankle. The guard went to kick him and fell flat on his face.

"That will teach you to pull someone's whiskers!" said Supercat.

James ran upstairs.

"Follow the signs to the exit, everyone. Head for the heliport."

They raced outside just in time

to see Count Backwards marching
towards his helicopter. It had a new
set of propellers. James looked at
his watch.

"It's five o'clock!" he gasped.

"Time flies when you're fighting
crime," said Supercat.

"It's the Count who's about to fly,"
said James. "If we let him go, he'll hit
France in less than an hour."

They ran towards the enemy
helicopter.

"Come back, Backwards!" shouted
Supercat.

The Count stuck out his tongue and climbed into the cockpit.

"You couldn't catch fleas!" he snickered. "You can't catch me, you furry fool!"

He started the engine. Supercat took a giant leap and hung on to the helicopter tail to try and stop it taking off, but even he wasn't heavy enough. The helicopter lifted into the air, but he clung on. Count Backwards spun the helicopter and shook him like a rug.

"Drop it, pussycat!" he cackled, spinning even faster.

Suddenly, Supercat lost his grip
with his left paw.

James was
hovering underneath,
but there was no
way he could catch
him if he fell from
such a great height.

"Hang on, Supercat!" he yelled.
"Left paw up a bit!"

But Supercat's cape had blown over his head. He couldn't see what he was doing. In his panic, he suddenly let go. James covered his eyes and waited for the thud.

187

"He flies through the air with greatest of ease…" sang Supercat.

James watched in wonder. Supercat's cape had filled with air like a parachute and he was floating gently down on to the runway.

As soon as he landed, James gave him a squeeze. He was so relieved.

"I thought you'd used up all nine of your lives that time, Supercat," he said.

"One down, eight to go!" said Supercat. "I will not rest until I catch Count Backwards."

"Nor me!" agreed James. "But I need to think of the best plan of action."

There was a whole fleet of helicopters lined up near the launch pad. He turned to Professor Sprout.

"Do you have a pilot's licence? As you're the only adult, we need you to shoot down the Count's helicopter before he drops more weevil bombs."

The professor went pale.

"You won't get me up in one of those things. I'm scared of heights. I fell out of my pram when I was a baby."

Supercat tapped James on the shoulder.

"Hello? I have superpowers, remember. Hold on to your hat, it's—"

"Yes, but you can't possibly man a

helicopter… can you?" said James.

Supercat narrowed his eyes.

"I'll do anything for a chip," he said. "Believe me, fur will fly!"

Supercat jumped into the nearest helicopter and strapped himself into the seat.

"I'll be co-pilot," said James.

"And I'll be hiding in the Gents until you get back," said Professor Sprout.

The helicopter whirred and lifted into the air. James checked the compass.

"Count Backwards is flying fifty degrees south."

"Not for long!" said Supercat, pulling on the controls.

They chased after the Count. He cursed them with a string of foul sums and sped off out of sight.

"Oh… *bulldogs*! We've lost him," said Supercat.

James studied the radar. Nothing… nothing… nothing…

"There he is!" he said. "Bring him down over the river. We don't want innocent people to get hurt."

"Will do!" said Supercat. "Which button launches missiles – this one?"

He gave it a prod. A woman burst into song.

"That's the radio," said James.

Supercat pressed another button. A blast of warm air shot up the tail hole in his costume.

"That's the heater," said James. "Try the red one."

Supercat thumped it with his paw.

193

Ack-ack-ack-ack-ack-ack-ack!

A stream of potatoes thundered out of the helicopter's giant spud gun.

"Third time lucky!" said James. "Keep firing, Supercat. Force Count Backwards forward."

Supercat was confused.

"Forward… Backwards? Make up your mind up."

"Engage him in a dogfight," said James.

Supercat's hackles went up.

"*Dog*fight? *Excusez-moi*, do I look like a dog?"

"This is no time to worry about your appearance," said James. "The Count's getting away. Go after him!"

"I'm doing it," said Supercat. "I'm doing it!"

He made a three-point turn and shot after the Count as he zigzagged ahead of them.

"You're on his tail!" said James. "Take aim… Fire!"

Supercat hit the red button.

Ack-ack-ack–ack-ack-ack-ack!

The Count dodged behind a big black cloud.

195

"Missed!" spat Supercat. "I'm almost out of ammo. Where's he gone? My flying goggles have steamed up."

James wiped the lenses on his sleeve.

"Better?"

The black cloud moved. Supercat's
tail bristled like a toilet brush.

"I see him!"

The Count was hovering over them

like a giant bird of prey. But before he had a chance to attack them, Supercat performed a daring death spiral and dropped out of sight.

"Great move!" said James.

"Great navigating!" said Supercat.

"Thanks," said James. "If we don't make it, I want you to know that I'm really glad I never swapped you for a crocodile… To your right! To your left… Aim… Fire!"

Ack-ack-ack-ack-ack!

A plume of smoke billowed out of the Count's helicopter.

198

"Got him!" whooped James. "He's going down!"

The enemy helicopter went into a nosedive, buzzed like a dying wasp and hit the surface of the water. They watched as it sank slowly beneath the river.

"Good riddance, Backwards!" cheered Supercat. "We shan't be seeing you again!"

"I wouldn't count on it," said James.

Chapter Eight

CHIP CHIP HURRAH!

Back at Wacko's Cut Brand factory, Professor Sprout was hiding in the Gents' toilet.

"You're safe to come out now, Professor," called James.

"Count Backwards sleeps with the fishes," said Supercat.

The professor flushed and opened the door.

"Does he? Chip chip hurrah! I'd love to see the look on the Calculators' faces when they find out – but of course they're not here."

Come to think of it, James and Supercat hadn't seen a single crew member since they got back.

"Where are they?" said James. "I thought it was quiet."

Professor Sprout gave a little smile.

"They've gone to weevil-bomb Belgium," he said. "But don't worry.

The helicopters will never get there.
I put sherbet in their fuel tanks."

"High five!" said Supercat, giving the professor's hand an enthusiastic biff. Professor Sprout stood there awkwardly.
He'd never been high-fived in his life, let alone by cat. Not knowing how to respond, he grasped Supercat's paw

and shook it.

"Well done, sir!" he said. "And you, James. Great teamwork."

He pulled out a notebook and showed them diagrams of the weevil-eating bugs he was about to breed.

"I'm going to the lab now," he said. "The sooner I start, the sooner they can save the potatoes."

"And the sooner the chip shops will reopen," said Supercat. "Home, James! Let's not hold Professor Sprout up a second longer."

"We need to go back to the farm first to fetch Dad's spuds," said James. "That's if you still want chips for tea?"

"Do bears poop in the woods?" said Supercat.

They linked arms and walked out of the factory.

"It still stinks of manure out here," said James.

"I think that's us," said Supercat. "Where's your bike?"

Luckily, it was still chained to the motor-castle porch. James didn't have a clue how to get home, but thanks to Supercat it wasn't a problem. He had cat-nav and, using his super-feline strength to pedal the BMX, they made it back to Murphy's Farm before dark. James collected the bucket of potatoes they had dug up earlier.

"There's enough here to keep us in chips for a fortnight," he said.

They wobbled home under the weight of spuds. Supercat parked the bike in the garden shed and went to go inside.

James stopped him just in time. "You need to take your costume off," he reminded him. "We don't want anyone to know you're Supercat, remember? Especially Mimi. Indoors, you are Tiger."

Supercat undressed and handed his clothes to James.

"And the pants," said James.

"Now I just look silly," said Supercat.

He got down on all fours.

"This is embarrassing," he said. "I've just rid the world of an evil villain," James smiled.

"You were brilliant," he said. "I'll never forget it, but if you could also remember to stop talking that would be really cool. Just meow and purr, OK?"

"Am I allowed to breathe?" groaned Supercat.

He followed James into the house. Dad was very pleased to see them back with his potatoes. But Mum wasn't happy.

"Phwoarr! What have you two been up to?" she said. "You stink."

Supercat wanted to say that they'd been busy defeating Count Backwards to save world peace, but James spoke up first.

"Tiger followed me to the farm. He fell in a pile of manure. I rescued him."

Mum pointed her potato peeler at Supercat.

"Give him a bath, James. And have one yourself. You can't eat in that state."

"I can eat in any state," grumbled Tiger as they went up to the bathroom.

Mimi was waiting for them on the stairs.

"Heard you talking, pussycat!" she

said, with an annoying grin.

James sat down next to her.

"Repeat after me," he said, "I'm a little mad girl. I think cats can talk."

"You're a little mad girl!" said Mimi.

Suddenly she spotted the pair of cat-sized pants that James had dropped. She snatched them and put her finger through the tail hole.

"Ha ha! I'm going to tell all your friends that your cat wears knickers," she said. "Unless… you let me put Tiger's fur in Mummy's hair rollers!"

After their baths, James came

down wearing hair gel. But Supercat
wore a big pink bow in his curly fur.

"Mimi, what have you done to that
poor animal?" said Mum.

"Ask him," said Mimi. "He can talk."

"Me… how?" said Supercat. "I
mean me-ow… meow… meow!"

James quickly changed the subject.
"Tiger meows like that when he's
hungry. Are the chips ready, Mum?"

They all sat in front of the telly
and ate them while they watched
the news.

"*Reports have come in about*

a helicopter fight over the river.

It happened this afternoon near

Wacko's Cut Brand ketchup

factory..."

"Good grief!" said Dad.

The report continued: "*A witness*

claimed that the pilot who was shot

down had numbers tattooed on his face. *He is believed to be a dangerous maniac, well known to the Secret Service, but they are refusing to release his name.*"

"Grrrr," growled Tiger.

"*So far, no one has identified the hero who flew the other helicopter. If you know who the pilot is, please call, as the Secret Service wishes to reward him for his bravery...*"

Supercat's paw shot up. Then, remembering that he had to be Tiger, he licked it and pretended he was washing his ears. James looked at him fondly. He really was the pet he'd always wanted. Supercat made wolves, bears and lions look tame.

"Forget Tigerman," he whispered. "*You're* my hero, Supercat."

"Anybody want more chips?" said Mum.

EPILOGUE

A week later, in a submarine somewhere deep under the river, a mysterious figure listened to the radio.

"And now for the latest news. The potato shortage is over. After a tip-off from a Mr S. Cat, detectives

have found tons of potatoes in a

castle belonging to Buck Daconstraw.

These have been delivered to chip

shops all over the country, which

will start frying them tonight.

Meanwhile, a top scientist has created

a bug which will destroy the potato-

munching weevils within days..."

In a fit of madness, the person
listening picked up the radio and
threw it out of the porthole, forgetting
that he was in a submarine. As the
water gushed in, he made a quick
calculation.

"I may not have five, four, three, two, won this time!" he gurgled. "But you can count on it, Supercat. Backwards will be baaaaaaack!"

THE ALL-ACTION CAT IS
BACK!

Tiger was an ordinary pet, until the day he licked a toxic sock and was transformed into… **SUPERCAT!**

Now the evil Count Backwards has kidnapped the Queen from her own birthday party and plans to take over the world! With his superpowers, his best friend James, and a few tricks in his party bag, can Supercat save the day?

It's party time...

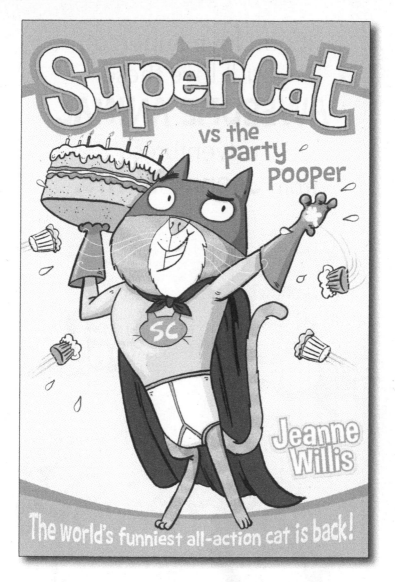

COMING SOON!

If you love Supercat,
you'll love these
AWESOME ANIMAL
adventures
from **Jeanne Willis:**

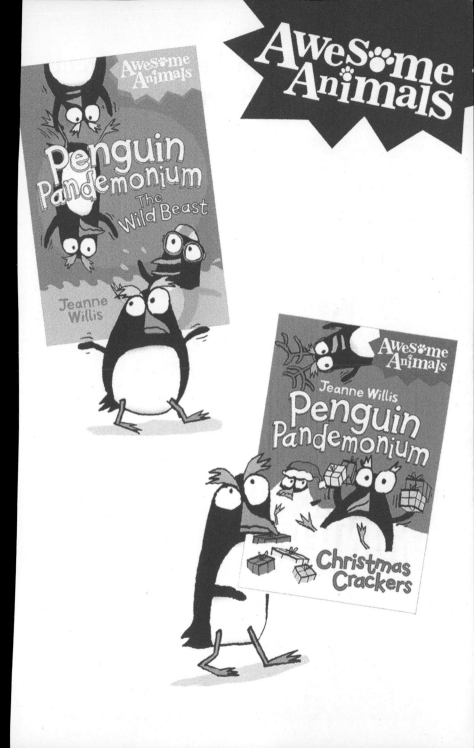

Get your **PAWS** on these other great books from **HarperCollins**:

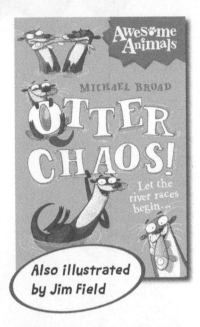